STARK LIBRARY

Dear Parents:

Congratulations! Your child is taking the first steps on an exciting journey. The destination? Independent reading!

STEP INTO READING® will help your child get there. The program offers five steps to reading success. Each step includes fun stories and colorful art or photographs. In addition to original fiction and books with favorite characters, there are Step into Reading Non-Fiction Readers, Phonics Readers and Boxed Sets, Sticker Readers, and Comic Readers—a complete literacy program with something to interest every child.

Learning to Read, Step by Step!

Ready to Read   Preschool–Kindergarten
• big type and easy words • rhyme and rhythm • picture clues
For children who know the alphabet and are eager to begin reading.

Reading with Help   Preschool–Grade 1
• basic vocabulary • short sentences • simple stories
For children who recognize familiar words and sound out new words with help.

Reading on Your Own   Grades 1–3
• engaging characters • easy-to-follow plots • popular topics
For children who are ready to read on their own.

Reading Paragraphs   Grades 2–3
• challenging vocabulary • short paragraphs • exciting stories
For newly independent readers who read simple sentences with confidence.

Ready for Chapters   Grades 2–4
• chapters • longer paragraphs • full-color art
For children who want to take the plunge into chapter books but still like colorful pictures.

STEP INTO READING® is designed to give every child a successful reading experience. The grade levels are only guides; children will progress through the steps at their own speed, developing confidence in their reading. The F&P Text Level on the back cover serves as another tool to help you choose the right book for your child.

Remember, a lifetime love of reading starts with a single step!

For Ms. Sheehan, a wonderful
teacher and friend
—A.P.

To Kimball Elementary
—S.K.

Visit us on the Web!
rhcbooks.com

Educators and librarians, for a variety of teaching tools,
visit us at RHTeachersLibrarians.com

Library of Congress Cataloging-in-Publication Data
Names: Penfold, Alexandra, author. | Kaufman, Suzanne, illustrator.
Title: All are welcome: give what you can / Alexandra Penfold; illustrated by Suzanne Kaufman.
Description: New York : Random House, 2023. | Audience: Ages 4–6.
Summary: Illustrations and simple, rhyming text introduce kids who work together to give
back to their community. | Identifiers: LCCN 2022047311 (print) | LCCN 2022047312 (ebook)
ISBN 978-0-593-43007-1 (paperback) | ISBN 978-0-593-43008-8 (library binding)
ISBN 978-0-593-43009-5 (ebook)
Subjects: CYAC: Stories in rhyme. | Generosity—Fiction. | Helpfulness—Fiction.
Communities—Fiction. | LCGFT: Stories in rhyme. | Picture books.
Classification: LCC PZ8.3.P376 Am 2023 (print) | LCC PZ8.3.P376 (ebook) |DDC [E]—dc23

Printed in the United States of America
10 9 8 7 6 5 4 3 2 1

This book has been officially leveled by using the F&P Text Level Gradient™ Leveling System.

STEP INTO READING®

STEP 2

READING WITH HELP

All Are Welcome

Give What You Can

by Alexandra Penfold

illustrated by Suzanne Kaufman

Random House 🏠 New York

If you see a need,

do a good deed.

BOOK
DONATION

Give what you can.

Then make a plan.

SEEDS

TOMATO

TURNIP

PUMPKIN

Start with a walk

and clean up the block!

Get together. Lend a hand.

Can we do it? Yes, we can!

Find the right space.

Create a new place.

First plant a seed.

Then water and weed.

Fix what you make.

Mend what you break.

Get together. Lend a hand.

Can we do it? Yes, we can!

Brighten someone's day.

Ask a new kid to play.

Mix and blend.

Help out a friend.

Gather a team.

Follow a dream.

PUMPKIN

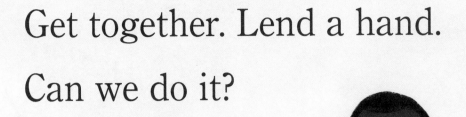

Get together. Lend a hand.
Can we do it?

Yes, we can!